For Zhéna

Eric Carle's DRAGONS DRAGONS
& other creatures that never were

compiled by Laura Whipple   *Philomel Books*

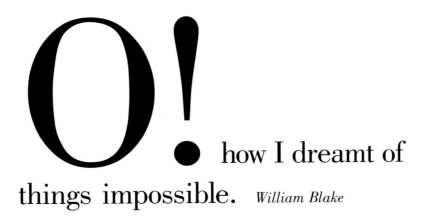

O! how I dreamt of things impossible. *William Blake*

8

Dragon

Oh, Tongue, give sound to joy and sing
of hope and promise on dragonwing!

Anne McCaffrey

Roc

Behold the sun
was suddenly hidden from me
and the air became
dull and dark. Methought a cloud
had come
over the sun. . .

I saw that the cloud
was none other than
an enormous bird
of gigantic girth and inordinately
wide of wing . . .

a huge bird,
called the Roc, which
feedeth its young
on elephants.

Sir Richard Burton

The Yeti

The Yeti is a manlike beast,
Unless, perchance, he doesn't exist.
He walks like a man and has hair on his face,
And rumors persist
That in forests and caves where no one goes,
Or high in the Himalayan snows,
He may still be living. Nobody knows.
If you meet him and ask him,
   "Are you a Yeti?"
All he can say is, "Maybe."

John Gardner

Minotaur

King Minos had a minotaur
   That all the people dreaded.
It gobbled fourteen kids a year,
   Incredibly bullheaded.

It dwelt inside a twisty maze
   That no one could escape
Till Theseus, shouting loud OLÉS!
   Swung sword and swished red cape.

X. J. Kennedy

Basilisk/Cockatrice

Head and body of a cock,
Its breath cracks rock.

Leather wings—Whish!
Serpent tail—Swish!
A Basilisk—Hisss!
No doodle-head this!

(A Basilisk!—HISSS!
Is also called—HISSS!
A Cockatrice.)

HISSSSSS!

Laura Whipple

Leviathan

He makes the deep to boil like a pot: he makes the sea
    like a pot of ointment, ointment in a mixing bowl.
He leaves a shining trail behind him, and in his wake
    the great river is like white hair.
Upon the earth there is not his like. . . .

The Book of Job

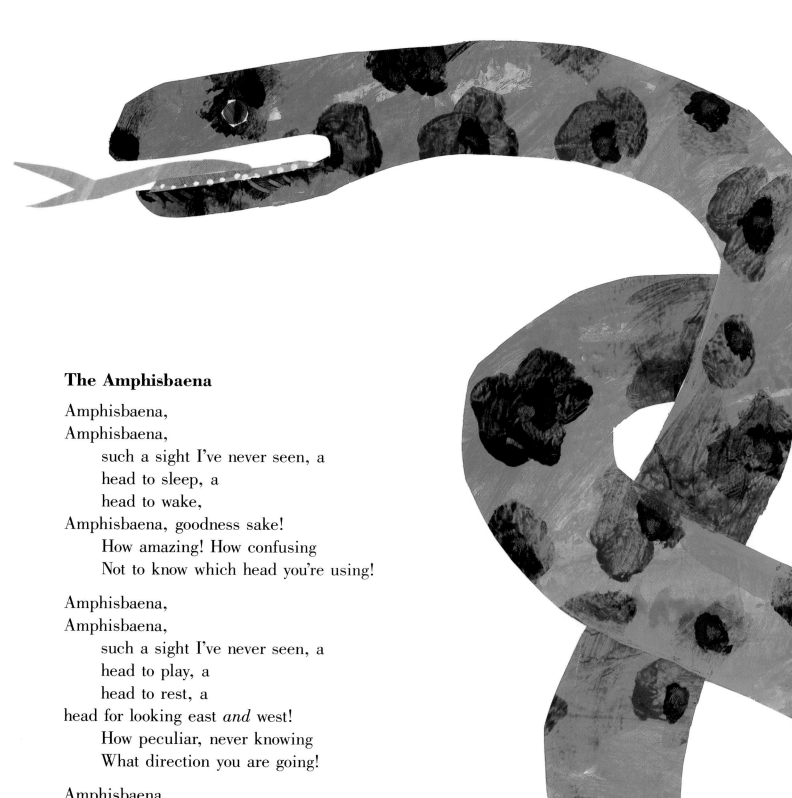

The Amphisbaena

Amphisbaena,
Amphisbaena,
 such a sight I've never seen, a
 head to sleep, a
 head to wake,
Amphisbaena, goodness sake!
 How amazing! How confusing
 Not to know which head you're using!

Amphisbaena,
Amphisbaena,
 such a sight I've never seen, a
 head to play, a
 head to rest, a
head for looking east *and* west!
 How peculiar, never knowing
 What direction you are going!

Amphisbaena,
Amphisbaena,
 such a sight I've never seen, a
 head to eat, a
 head to drink, a
head to talk, a head to think!
 Amphisbaena, what a trouble
 When you have to do things double!

      Myra Cohn Livingston

18

White Buffalo Woman

. . . A beautiful maiden dressed in sage
. . . unwrapped the pipe
and taught the songs and prayers
of five great ceremonies. . . .
She disappeared,
and the people saw only
a white buffalo cow
trotting over the prairie.

John Bierhorst

Rainbow Crow

I will go. I will stop the snow.

Aiya, aiya, aiya, aiya,
Rain, Rainbow Crow,
Stop the snow, Crow.
Fly to the sky high,
Rain, Rainbow Crow,
Aiya, aiya, aiya, aiya.

Nancy Van Laan

The Phoenix

(a poem for two voices)

I am Phoenix	I am Phoenix the fire-bird!
Phoenix everlasting! I am Phoenix!	Phoenix I am Phoenix! Immortal
Immortal eternal . . .	eternal undying . . .

My feathers are
   scarlet,
     purple,
     golden.
	scarlet,
	purple.

one	There is but one Phoenix—
there have never been more.	

Paul Fleishman

The Griffin

Protector of Pharaohs,
Defender of Kings,
The Griffin watched over
Their Crowns and their Rings,
With Wings of an Eagle,
And sharp Lion claws,
It once tore to pieces
The Breaker of Laws.
It heard every whisper,
And knew every plot
And you may believe it,
Or else you may not!

Arnold Sundgaard

The Hippogriff

When Mare and Griffin meet and mate
Their offspring share a curious fate.
One half is Horse with hooves and tail,
The rest is Eagle, claws and nail.
As a Horse it likes to graze
In summer meadows doused in haze,
Yet as an Eagle it can fly
Above the clouds where dreams drift by.
With such a Beast I am enthralled,
The Hippogriff this Beast is called.

Arnold Sundgaard

25

The Unicorn

Oh this is the animal that never was.
They hadn't seen one; but just the same, they loved
its graceful movement, the way it stood
looking at them calmly, with clear eyes. . . .

Rainer Maria Rilke

Pan

Sweet, sweet, sweet, O Pan!
  Piercing sweet by the river!
Blinding sweet, O great god Pan!
  The sun on the hill forgot to die,
And the lilies revived, and the dragon-fly
  Came back to dream on the river.

Elizabeth Barrett Browning

Kappa

Saucer on his head, carapace on his back,
the "river urchin" pulls pranks,
tickling your tush in the slimy lake,
stealing your bellybutton while you're snoozing.

But water is the source of his life.
When, out on land too long, his saucer
begins to dry, he dashes home
to keep his carapace cucumber-fresh.

Hiro Sato

The Centaurs

Playing upon the hill three centaurs were!
They lifted each a hoof! They stared at me!
And stamped the dust!

In furious brotherhood! Around, about,
They charged, they swerved, they leaped! Then, bound
　　on bound,
They raced into the wood!

James Stephens

Mermaid/Undersea

Beneath the waters
   Green and cool
The mermaids keep
   A swimming school.

The oysters trot;
   The lobsters prance;
The dolphins come
   To join the dance.

But all the jellyfish
   Who are rather small,
Can't seem to learn
   The steps at all.

Marchette Chute

Sphinx

As the sun
Is going down,
And shadows mix
With yellow sand,
He rises slowly,
Stretches, stands,
Wades into the Nile to wash

Mummy-dust and sand fleas off—
Licks heavy paws
With heavy tongue
Until the cool night air is gone.
While on Egyptian earth
He drops dry purrs,
Ground out like powdered rock.

Deborah Chandra

Pegasus

He could not be captured,
He could not be bought,
His running was rhythm,
His standing was thought;
With one eye on sorrow
And one eye on mirth,
He galloped in heaven
And gambolled on earth

And only the poet
With wings to his brain
Can mount him and ride him
Without any rein,
The stallion of heaven,
The steed of the skies,
The horse of the singer
Who sings as he flies.

Eleanor Farjeon

Bunyip

"What do bunyips look like?" asked the bunyip.

"Horrible," said the wallaby. "They have webbed feet and feathers."

"Fine handsome feathers," said the bunyip hopefully.

"Horrible feathers," said the wallaby firmly . . .

"Handsome webbed feet?" called the bunyip, but there was no answer.

"Can you please tell me what bunyips look like?"

"Yes," said the man. . . . "Bunyips don't look like anything. . . .
Bunyips simply don't exist."

The bunyip was shaken. . . .

"What a pity," he murmured. "What a pity, what a pity."

Jenny Wagner

Garuda

He perches in the dusty tamarind tree,
Once a blazing bird of light, part man,
And preens his fading wings remembering
How he bore Lord Vishnu over lands.

Resting ancient arms and tired claws,
He nestles warm within the jungle air,
And into thick green shadows of the leaves,
Feather by bright feather, disappears.

Deborah Chandra

Quetzalcoatl

In the world's young days,
Farmer met Quetzalcoatl in a field
by one rustling plant.
Like the wind,
he whispered in Farmer's ear,
This is my gift to you.
Its leaves are more precious
than green plumes,
its heart richer than jade.
Farmer asked, "What is its name?"
And the Serpent whispered,
Maize.

Tony Johnston

Kracken

Neath icelocked waves the Kracken lies
    In wait for passing ships,
To gobble them as you or I
    Might munch potato chips.

        X. J. Kennedy

Cerberus

There!
That terrible three-necked
hound
Cerberus crouched. . . .
Baying savagely from
his triple throat . . .
he barred the way to Pluto's house.

N. B. Taylor

Chimera

Do you always act polite?
Or would you *dare* a
Chi*mera* to fight? You might,
but you'd regret it, because
he isn't a *He*, he's an *Us*,
and all three heads are dangerous.

But look: Here comes Bellerophon
upon the winged horse Pegasus.

Big deal, he says,
Mr. Lion/goat/snake,
You're a silly mistake.
You have too many heads,
you can't be real,
you don't exist.

And with one twist of his magic sword,
he turned that Chimera into a *word*.

Penelope Scambly Schott

53

The Hippocamp

Oh, fabrous horse that's half a fish,
From stem to stern it's of a piece,
The Hippocamp, brave finny god,
Once roamed the seas of ancient Greece.

Who else dared trample down the waves
With scary scaly tail to swish,
Who swam and galloped all at once,
Fulfilling every fish's wish.

But is it creature or is it myth
Engraved upon a monolith?

Arnold Sundgaard

Anansi the Spider

Anansi.
He is "spider"
to the Ashanti people.

In Ashanti land,
people love . . . Kwaku Anansi.

This funny fellow is a rogue, a wise and
lovable trickster. He is a
shrewd and cunning
figure. . . .
Anansi is a mischief maker.
He tumbles into
many troubles.

Gerald McDermott

Okolo the Leopard Warrior

HE COMES! . . .

Towering in majesty over the people,
Okolo has come from the heart of the forest,
the leopard warrior, young and strong.

He stands there in glory,
and then he is gone!

The Lord of the Beasts
has gone back to the forest,
swift as a leopard
that leaps on its prey.

Christine Price

The Manticore

A mythic beast, the manticore—
Dragon behind and man before,
With lion sandwiched in between 'em.
No living soul has ever seen him,
Nor any combination of
The creatures in the list above.

Jeanne Steig

Dragon

Let me tell you about me.
Children love me,
You're a child.
All my heads are green and handsome.
All my eyes are red and wild.
All my toes have claws upon them.
All the claws have hooks.
I blow smoke through all my noses.
It is hotter than it looks.
All my tails have points upon them.
All my teeth are sharp and blue.
I won't bite you very badly.
I am fond of you.
All my scales are shaped like arrows.
They will hurt you if you touch.
So, although I know you love me,
Do not pet me very much.

Karla Kuskin

If we shadows have offended,
Think but this, and all is mended,
That you have but slumber'd here,
While these visions did appear.
And this weak and idle theme,
No more yielding but a dream. . . .

William Shakespeare/A Midsummer Night's Dream

Introduction to the Glossary

Fabulous beasts with wing and fin and scale and fur have been found in myths and folklore for thousands of years. They fly, breathe fire and guard treasures. Carry heroes and gods. Threaten and save, trick and thoroughly mystify us. They are a magical part of our human heritage.

What remarkable human ingenuity and creativity formed these beasts! Joseph Campbell in *The Power of Myth* says that myths help put our minds in touch with the natural world and being alive. Some say these creatures come down to us through an ancient filter for understanding the power of nature. The dragon, breathing fire and smoke, dives from the sky like fallout from a volcanic eruption. In the first recorded description of a unicorn, the likeness to a rhinoceros is inescapable. And so on.

Certainly, the mythological creatures that are an amalgam of human and animal bodies represent the dual nature of our lives. Their violence, greed, anger, and even the devouring of others are an allegory of our darker side. Frequently, these dark beasts are slain by human heroes or induced to self-destruct. Message: evil can be conquered, even our own. More often, our finest attributes are illuminated by theirs: sacrifice of self for others, respect for purity, reverence for life, cleverness, wisdom, poetic inspiration, benevolence, helpfulness in time of adversity, attributes engaged in journeys of birth, struggle, death and rebirth. This is the very fabric of myth and yes, reflects the best of ourselves.

In these modern days when children's cultural heroes come from cartoon characters and the movies, we need to open their imaginations to these older performers. Let us allow our children to revel in the power and mystery of these magical creatures. Let them dream of things impossible.

Laura Whipple

Amphisbaena (am fis bee′nah)
European, North American—a serpent with a head at each end of its body. It could loop itself and roll like a hoop by putting one head into the jaws of the other. Some say it appeared in Massachusetts in the colony's early days.

Anansi (ah nahn′si)
African, Caribbean—a clever spider who has human qualities. Anansi, a folk hero in West Africa, appears in some stories as a human who has spider abilities, a real spiderman, sometimes wise, sometimes foolish, and always mischievous.

Basilisk (ba′szil isk)
European—also called cockatrice (kok′a tris). Considered the king of serpents, its fiery breath could burst stone and its evil glance could kill. It could be destroyed by forcing it to look at its own reflection. The basilisk was said to be born from a rooster's egg, hatched by a toad.

Bunyip (bun′yip)
Australian—a mythical creature of waterways and billibongs (stagnant pools). Its appearance is most often characterized as being unknown. Nevertheless, it has been described as dark with long fur or feathers, with and without horns and legs, oval shaped, web-footed, both large and small, with glowing eyes and a loud bellow.

Centaur (sen′tawr)
Greek—a hybrid creature. In Greek mythology, the centaurs were the offspring of Ixion, king of Thessaly, and a cloud. Followers of Dionysus, a god of fertility, they were regarded as uncouth and savage, though some became teachers of human beings.

Cerberus (sur′bur us)
Greek, Roman—the watchdog at the gates of Hades who allowed only the dead to pass. He was said to have three or more heads and jaws dripping with poisonous foam. Some say he had snakes growing from behind his neck and along his back or that his tail was a snake.

Chimera (ki mir′uh)
Greek—a hybrid lion. Although pictured with a lion's mane, the chimera was considered female. The Greek hero Bellerophon, riding upon the winged horse Pegasus, did battle with her and slew her.

Dragon (dra′gun)
Worldwide—a scaly lizardlike serpent of various types and sizes, with one to many heads, wings or no wings, legs or no legs. Some can talk with humans and many guard treasure. Western dragons are fierce, powerful, wise, and miserly. They breathe fire and are generally destructive. Oriental dragons are fierce, powerful, wise, and rich, but also quite benevolent. They breathe mist instead of fire.

Ganesha (gan eesh′a)
Indian—a minor god of the Hindu religion. Ganesha embodies success, prosperity, wisdom, peace, and the good life. A very popular figure in modern Hindu festival parades, Ganesha rides upon a rat.

Garuda (ga roo′da)
Indian—the Hindu mythological mount for the god Vishnu. Garuda is associated with the sun and symbolizes swiftness and strength. He is a destroyer of serpents and can cure snake bites.

Griffin (gri′fin)
European and Middle Eastern—a composite creature with the body of a lion, head of an eagle, and large, pointed ears that allow the griffin to

hear exceptionally well. A dangerous foe, it guards treasure and gold and is a hater of horses. It lays jewels instead of eggs in a cliff-top nest.

Hippocamp (hip′uh kamp)
Greek—a marvelous seahorse with the lower body of a dolphin. In various sources it has a serpent's tail. It pulled the chariot of Poseidon, god of the sea.

Hippogriff (hip′uh grif)
European and Middle Eastern—the offspring of a horse and a griffin. It lives in mountainous regions, and when not in the air, grazes on grasses. It appears in the poetry of Virgil and is a symbol of poetic inspiration.

Kappa (ka′pah)
Japanese—a water-dwelling trickster the size of a boy. The kappa is said to have spiky hair surrounding a saucer-shaped depression in its head which holds water and is the source of its considerable strength. A lover of wrestling and cucumbers, it gives off a fishy smell. People in lakes and rivers need to watch out for the kappa as it will maliciously drag them under.

Kracken (kra′ken)
Norwegian—a round, somewhat flat, floating sea monster large enough to be mistaken by sailors for an island. It causes whirlpools, and when it sinks beneath the waves, it engulfs any ship in the area.

Leviathan (le vi′a thun)
Biblical—the monstrous sea creature from the Book of Job in the Old Testament.

Manticore (man′tih kor)
Middle Eastern—a powerful creature with the body of a lion, the head of a man, a tail with the spikes of a scorpion's stinger, and an oversized mouth with three rows of shark-sharp teeth. It especially liked to eat humans. The manticore could not be fenced or walled in since it could jump to great heights.

Mermaid (mur′made)
Greek, European—a water being. Some stories say a mermaid had two tails or legs and could change into a real woman and live as a human on land until the sea called for her return. Mermaids known as sirens lured sailors with their singing to a watery death or a new life under the sea.

Minotaur (min′uh tawr)
Greek—a half bull, half man who was imprisoned in a Cretan labyrinth built by Daedalus, the architect. Minos, king of Crete, demanded a yearly tribute of young men and women from Athens to feed this monster. It was finally slain in the labyrinth by the Athenian hero Theseus.

Okolo (oh koh′loh)
Nigerian—a legendary leopard warrior of the Yoruba tribe represented in a ceremonial dance mask.

Pan
Greek—the god of woodland and meadow, shepherds and flocks. Half man and half goat, Pan was musical and invented the shepherd's pipe. Pan is sometimes used as a symbol of the universe and the natural world.

Pegasus (peg′uh sus)
Greek, Roman—a winged horse born from the blood of Medusa when she was slain by Perseus. Pegasus carried the hero Bellerophon in his battle with the Chimera. Some myths say springs rose where Pegasus' hooves touched the earth. He was the horse of the Muses, connected to poetry.

Phoenix (fee′nix)
Egyptian, Middle Eastern, Asian—a mythical bird. It lived to a great age reported to be from 500 to 7000 years. At the end of its life, it burned itself in a nest of flames and was born again. Rising from its own ashes, it is a symbol of immortality.

Quetzalcoatl (ket sal koh at′l)
Mexican, American Indian—the plumed serpent god of Toltec, Aztec, and other North American Indian tribes. He was identified with the wind and with great moral principles and respect for life. He taught the people writing, painting, and dancing, how to raise corn and cotton, and how to work with gold, metal, and wood.

Rainbow Crow
North American Indian—a heroic crow of a Lenape tribe myth. To save the animals from winter, it flew to the Great Spirit in the Sky and brought back the gift of fire. Ever since then, the multicolored feathers of Rainbow Crow have been covered with soot, and his beautiful voice has been hoarse from the ashes he swallowed while carrying the flaming stick in his beak.

Roc (rok)
Middle Eastern—the Arabic bird from the Sinbad tales and the tales of Marco Polo. This gigantic bird of prey had such prodigious strength, it transported elephants in its talons to feed its nesting young. The story says the eggs were as large as the dome of a mosque.

Sphinx (sfinks)
Greek, Egyptian, Middle Eastern—a fabulous beast found in several mythologies. In Egypt, where it guarded tombs and temples, it had a man's head and was a symbol of the god Horus. The Greek sphinx was female and lived on the rocks above the city of Thebes. She devoured all passersby who could not answer the riddle she posed.

Unicorn (yoo′nuh korn)
European, Asian—a magical horse with a twisted horn growing from its forehead and the beard of a goat. First described in Pliny as a ferocious beast with the feet of an elephant, it has evolved through the ages into a more benevolent and appealing creature. The medieval version pictures it as a pure white horse of great strength and beauty, which can be captured only by an innocent young maiden.

White Buffalo Woman
American Indian—the mythic white buffalo who came in the guise of a young woman to the Lakota Sioux tribe to teach and guide the people in times of trouble.

Yeti (yeh′tee)
Asian—the Himalayan abominable snowman, an apelike creature from the highest reaches of the mountains. It supposedly walks upright like a human, and the Sherpas of Nepal report many sightings. The yeti is pictured in Tibetan scrolls and manuscripts.

No glossary can paint a precise picture of the likes of chimeras and dragons and basilisks. These marvelous creations can never be described definitively. Accounts of their appearance vary from source to source and tale to tale. It is appropriate that their images shift slightly in our minds with the storytelling of the moment.

Copyright Acknowledgments

Philomel Books would like to thank the following for permission to reprint the selections in this book. All possible care has been taken to trace the ownership of every selection included and to make full acknowledgment for its use. If any errors have accidentally occurred, they will be corrected in subsequent editions provided notification is sent to the publishers:

John Bierhorst: "White Buffalo Woman" from a Lakota Sioux legend as told by Elk Head, 1907, from *The Mythology of North America* by John Bierhorst. Copyright © 1985 by John Bierhorst. Published by William Morrow and Company.

Deborah Chandra: "Garuda" and "Sphinx" by Deborah Chandra. Copyright © 1991 by Deborah Chandra. Printed by permission of the author.

Marchette Chute: "Undersea" by Marchette Chute. Reprinted by permission of Mary Chute Smith for the author.

Eleanor Farjeon: "Pegasus" from *The Children's Bells* by Eleanor Farjeon. Copyright © 1969 by Eleanor Farjeon. Published by Oxford University Press. Reprinted by permission of David Higham Associates Limited.

Paul Fleishman: "The Phoenix: a poem for two voices" from *I Am Phoenix, Poems for Two Voices*. Copyright © 1985 by Paul Fleishman. Reprinted by permission of HarperCollins Publishers.

John Gardner: "The Yeti" from *A Child's Bestiary* by John Gardner. Copyright © 1977 by Boskydell Artists, Ltd. Reprinted by permission of Georges Borchardt, Inc. for the Estate of John Gardner.

Tony Johnston: "Quetzalcoatl" by Tony Johnston. Copyright © 1991 by Tony Johnston. Printed by permission of the author.

Hiro Sato: "Kappa" by Hiro Sato. Copyright © 1991 by Hiro Sato. Printed by permission of the author.

Penelope Scambly Schott: "Chimera" by Penelope Scambly Schott. Copyright © 1991 by Penelope Scambly Schott. Printed by permission of the author.

Jeanne Steig: "The Manticore" from *Consider the Lemming* by Jeanne Steig. Copyright © 1988 by Jeanne Steig. Reprinted by permission of Farrar, Strauss and Giroux, Inc.

James Stephens: Stanzas one and four from "The Centaurs" by James Stephens. Acknowledgment is made to the Society of Authors on behalf of the copyright holder, Mrs. Iris Wise.

Arnold Sundgaard: "The Griffin," "The Hippocamp," and "The Hippogriff" by Arnold Sundgaard. Copyright © 1991 by Arnold Sundgaard. Printed by permission of the author.

N.B. Taylor: "Cerberus" from *The Aeneid of Virgil*, retold by N.B. Taylor. Copyright © 1961. Published by Henry Z. Walck.

Nancy Van Laan: "Rainbow Crow" from *Rainbow Crow*, retold by Nancy Van Laan. Text Copyright © 1989 by Nancy Van Laan. Reprinted by permission of Alfred A. Knopf, Inc.

Jenny Wagner: "Bunyip" an excerpt from *The Bunyip of Berkeley's Creek* by Jenny Wagner. Copyright © 1973 by Ron Brooks and Childerset. Reprinted by permission of Penguin Books Australia Ltd.

X.J. Kennedy: "Kracken" "Minotaur" from *Did Adam Name the Vinegaroon?* by X.J. Kennedy. Copyright © 1982 by X.J. Kennedy. Reprinted by permission of David R. Godine, Publisher.

Karla Kuskin: "Dragon" from *Any Me I Want to Be* by Karla Kuskin. Copyright © 1972 by Karla Kuskin. Reprinted by permission of HarperCollins Publishers.

Myra Cohn Livingston: "Amphisbaena" by Myra Cohn Livingston. Copyright © 1973 by Myra Cohn Livingston. Appeared originally in *Cricket* Magazine. Reprinted by permission of Marion Reiner for the author.

"Ganesha, Ganesh" by Myra Cohn Livingston. Copyright © 1991 by Myra Cohn Livingston. Printed by permission of Marian Reiner for the author.

Anne McCaffrey: "Dragon" from *Dragonsong* by Anne McCaffrey. Copyright © 1976 by Anne McCaffrey. Reprinted with permission of Atheneum Books for Young Readers, an imprint of Simon & Schuster Children's Publishing Division.

Gerald McDermott: "Anansi the Spider" from *Anansi the Spider, a tale from the Ashanti* by Gerald McDermott. Copyright © 1972 by Landmark Productions Incorporated. Reprinted by permission of Henry Holt and Company, Inc.

Christine Price: "Okolo the Leopard Warrior" from *Dancing Masks of Africa* by Christine Price. Copyright © 1975 by Christine Price. Reprinted with permission of Atheneum Books for Young Readers, an imprint of Simon & Schuster Children's Publishing Division.

Rainer Maria Rilke: "Unicorn" from *The Selected Poetry of Rainer Maria Rilke*, edited and translated by Stephen Mitchell. Copyright © 1982 by Stephen Mitchell. Reprinted by permission of Random House, Inc.

Laura Whipple: "Basilisk/Cockatrice" by Laura Whipple. Copyright © 1991 by Laura Whipple. Printed by permission of the author.

Robert Wyndham: "Chinese Dragon" from *Chinese Mother Goose Rhymes*, edited by Robert Wyndham. Copyright © 1968 by Robert Wyndham. Reprinted by permission of Philomel Books.

Eric Carle prepares his own colored tissue papers. Different textures are achieved by using various brushes to splash, spatter, and finger-paint acrylic paints onto thin tissue papers. These colored tissue papers then become his palette. They are cut or torn into shapes as needed and are glued onto white illustration board. Some areas of his designs, however, are painted directly on the board before the bits of tissue paper are applied to make the collage illustration.

Laura Whipple, who collected the poems for this special anthology, is an elementary school media specialist and a graduate of Rutgers University Graduate School of Communication, Information, and Library Studies.

Published in 1991 by Philomel Books,
a division of The Putnam & Grosset Group,
200 Madison Avenue, New York, NY 10016.
Illustrations copyright © 1991 by the Eric Carle Corporation.
Compilation copyright © 1991 by Philomel Books.
All rights reserved. This book, or parts thereof, may not be reproduced in any form without permission in writing from the publisher.
Philomel Books, Reg. U.S. Pat. & Tm. Off.
Sandcastle and the Sandcastle logo are trademarks
belonging to The Putnam & Grosset Group.
First Sandcastle edition 1996. Published simultaneously in Canada.
Printed and bound in Hong Kong. The text is set in Bodoni Book.

Library of Congress Cataloging-in-Publication Data
Carle, Eric. [Dragons dragons and other creatures that never were]
Eric Carle's dragons dragons and other creatures that never were / compiled by Laura Whipple.
p. cm. Includes index.
Summary: An illustrated collection of poems about dragons and other fantastic creatures by a variety of authors.
ISBN (hardcover) 0-399-22105-0
10 9 8 7 6 5 4 3
ISBN (Sandcastle) 0-399-22837-3
10 9 8 7 6 5

ALTERNATE:

Copyright Acknowledgments

Dragon Dragons

Printed in Hong Kong